SALT

A RUSSIAN FOLKTALE

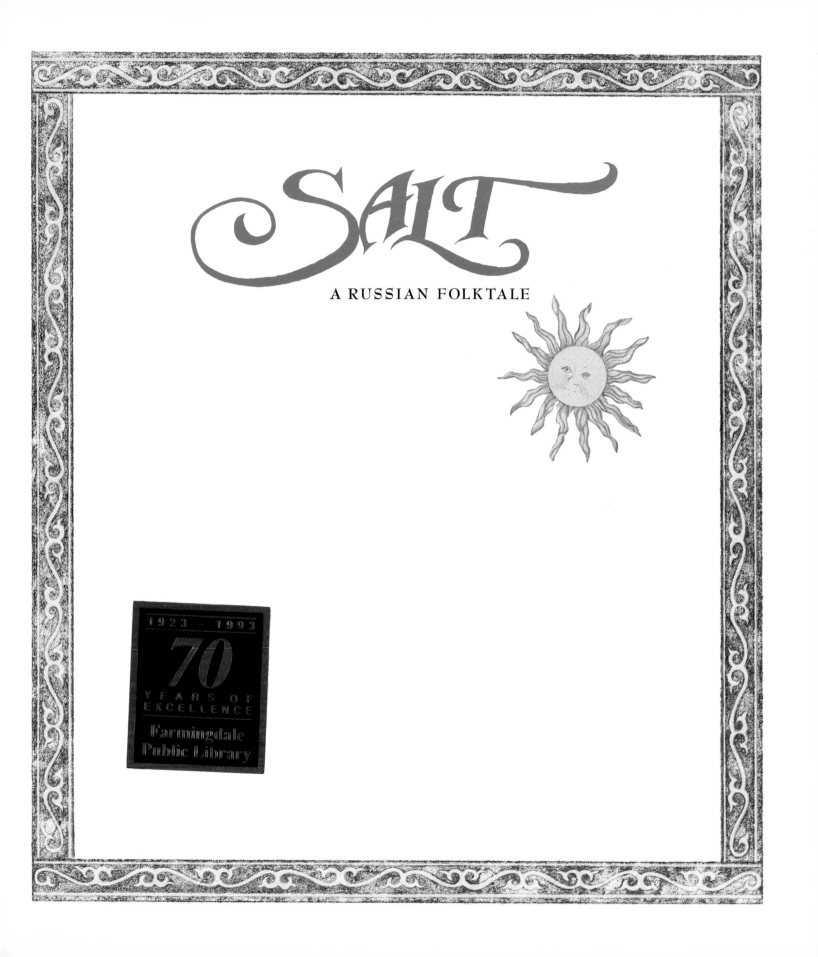

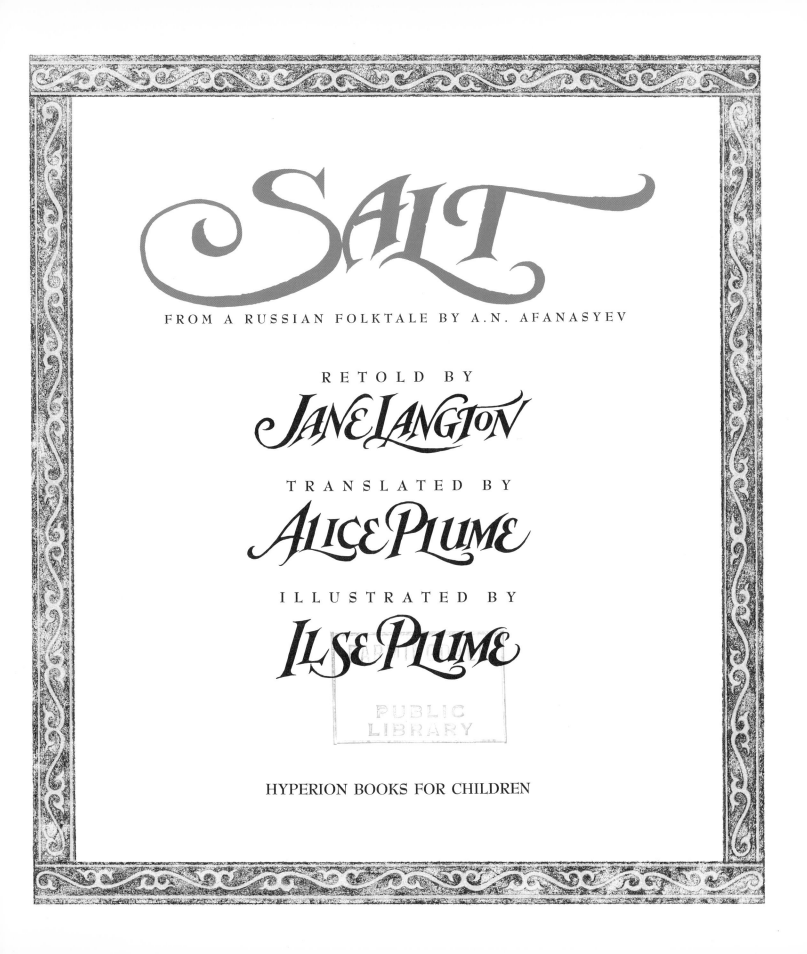

SALT

FROM A RUSSIAN FOLKTALE BY A.N. AFANASYEV

RETOLD BY

Jane Langton

TRANSLATED BY

Alice Plume

ILLUSTRATED BY

Ilse Plume

HYPERION BOOKS FOR CHILDREN

Library of Congress Cataloging-in-Publication Data
Langton, Jane.
Salt: a Russian folktale / retold by Jane Langton; translated by
Alice Plume; illustrated by Ilse Plume.
p.   cm.
Translated from Russian.
Summary: Ivan, the merchant's third son, having patience and an
eye for opportunity, barters the cargo of his ship for a princess
and a fortune.
ISBN 1-56282-178-4 (trade) — ISBN 1-56282-179-2 (lib. bdg.)
[1. Folklore — Soviet Union.]   I. Plume, Alice.   II. Plume, Ilse,
ill.   III. Title.
PZ8.1.L27Sal   1992
398.21 — dc20
[E]   91-74007   CIP   AC

The artwork for each picture is prepared with colored pencils on Strathmore paper.
This book is set in 14-point Bernhard Modern.

To Liz Gordon, with appreciation and admiration…
Ilse Plume

For Colin…
Jane Langton

SALT

A RUSSIAN FOLKTALE

There is an island in the sea—
not too near, not too far—
where stands a tree with a golden top.
On this tree sits a purring cat...
on a golden chain.
When he goes up, he sings a song,
and when he comes down, he tells a story.
Now the cat is coming down.
The story lies before you.

Once there was a merchant who had three sons. The two oldest, Fyodor and Vasily, were clever, but the third was called Ivan the Fool because, although he was a good-looking young man, he asked so many silly questions.

"Is the world round or flat?" he asked his father.

"It is flat, of course," said his father impatiently. "Everyone knows that."

"How high is the sky?" asked Ivan.

"As high as the church steeple," said his father angrily. "Now stop asking questions. You are a foolish boy."

The merchant was rich. He owned many ships, and he sent them out all over the world with valuable cargoes.

One day he loaded his finest ship with furs—wolf and fox and sable—and ordered his men to mount on board a pair of shining cannons. Then he called his eldest son and said, "Fyodor, take these furs across the sea to the kingdoms of the far north and sell them for gold and silver and jewels."

Next he filled his swiftest ship with a cargo of gleaming ice and said to his second son, "Vasily, you must sail to the cities of the south, where the weather is hot, and sell your cargo for gold and silver and jewels. But you must make haste, or the ice will melt on the way." And he gave his son a sharp sword.

The youngest son, Ivan the Fool, went up into a tall tower overlooking the harbor and saw the sails of his father's two handsome ships fill with air and quiver, as if they were eager to fly before the wind. He watched until the two ships were out of sight.

Now, he thought, it is *my* turn. He went to his father and asked to be sent out to sea in another of his father's ships.

"No, no," said his father. "You are too foolish. I cannot trust you with such an important journey."

But Ivan begged and pleaded, and at last his father agreed. He gave him the smallest ship in his fleet and loaded it, not with precious furs or with ice that flashed like diamonds but with a cargo of wooden spoons. He gave Ivan a knife with a blade only an inch long.

But Ivan was glad. He went on board the small ship, and soon the sailors were climbing the mast, spreading the sails, and running up a bright flag from the masthead.

Ivan thrust the little knife in his belt and tucked a wooden spoon in his pocket. Now, he said to himself, I will learn the height of the sky. I will find out if the world is round or flat.

The little ship set forth, rocking smoothly on the waves. Time went by—not too much, not too little—when suddenly a storm came whistling out of the north.

"We must find a safe harbor," said Ivan, and at once he made for an island where a white mountain rose out of the sea.

"How strange," cried the sailors, "a mountain of snow!"

But when Ivan dipped his finger in the snow and tasted it, he said, "It is not snow, it is salt. Salt is more precious than wooden spoons! Without salt there is no savor."

As soon as the storm was over, he ordered his men to dump the wooden spoons into the sea and fill the barrels with salt from the mountain.

The sailors hurried to do his bidding. Soon the spoons were drifting away on the tide, and the barrels were full of salt.

Once more Ivan set sail, looking for a port where he could sell his new cargo and bring back riches to his father, to prove that he, Ivan the Fool, was not so foolish after all.

Before long the ship arrived at a fine harbor where a wealthy tsar ruled a rich land.

Putting a bag of salt in his pocket, Ivan stepped down from the ship and strolled through the streets of the town. There were many people on the street with kopecks jingling in their purses. They were buying amber beads and gingerbread and baskets of mushrooms and holy icons and singing birds in cages. But Ivan went straight to the palace of the tsar to ask permission to sell his salt.

He found the tsar in the company of his daughter, the tsarevna. She was a beauty, a handsome girl with a golden braid. Her loveliness cannot be told in a tale, nor described with a pen. Ivan's heart jumped in his breast.

But the tsarevna did not look well. She was thin and sad. Ivan pulled at the sleeve of one of the tsar's servants. "Why is the tsarevna unhappy? Is she ill?"

"You ask too many questions," said the servant. But then he told Ivan that Tsarevna Marushka had stopped eating. "The tsar keeps hiring new cooks, but still the tsarevna complains that the food has no taste. If she does not eat soon, she will starve."

Ivan bowed down before the tsar and his lovely daughter. "My Lord," he said, "I wish to sell my goods in your country."

"What sort of goods are they?" asked the tsar. But he did not look at Ivan. Instead he looked anxiously at his daughter, who sat feebly in her chair. Her head was bent, but she glanced up at Ivan as he rose from his low bow and stood before her father.

"It is salt, my Lord." Ivan took the little bag from his pocket and poured salt into his hand and held it out for the tsar to see.

The tsar looked at the white grains. "Salt? What is salt? I see only white sand. We have plenty of sand in our country, little brother. We do not need to pay for it."

But he invited Ivan to stay for the evening meal, since he had come from a far country.

Ivan thanked the tsar and put the salt back in his pocket. Then he made his way to the kitchen to watch the cooks prepare the dinner.

In the kitchen there was great confusion. The cooks were running back and forth, trying to make something so delicious that the hungry tsarevna would eat it. Ivan watched as they roasted a goose and poured gravy into a bowl and sliced cabbages and onions into a pot of soup.

But something was missing. "When are you going to add salt?" he asked the head cook.

"Salt?" said the cook. "What is salt?"

"You mean you have never heard of salt? Don't you know that without salt there is no savor?"

The cook did not like advice from a stranger. "You ask too many questions," he said, and then he pushed Ivan out of the way with a tray of pudding.

Later on, when all the cooks were busy polishing the silver, Ivan took the bag of salt out of his pocket, sprinkled some of it into the soup, and stirred it in with his wooden spoon.

At dinnertime he sat at the far end of the table and watched the tsarevna as the cooks brought in the salted soup. At once she raised her bowed head and smiled. "How good it smells!" she said, and soon she was eating a big bowlful.

The tsar was pleased. "This soup is indeed more delicious than anything I have ever tasted," he said. He called the head cook from the kitchen and asked what he had put in the soup to make it taste so good.

"My Lord," said the bewildered cook, "I made it as I have always made it."

Then Ivan rose to his feet in triumph. "It is the salt, my Lord. I added some of my salt to the pot. The cook made a fine soup, but without salt there is no savor."

The tsar was overjoyed. "I will buy your salt. How much do you ask for all the salt in your ship?"

"Let us trade barrel for barrel. For three barrels of salt, I will take one of gold, one of silver, and one of precious stones. And one more thing." Ivan glanced at the smiling tsarevna, who was helping herself to a second bowl of soup. "I would like to marry your daughter."

The tsar was astonished. But Tsarevna Marushka jumped up from her chair and took Ivan's hand. "Father," she said, "I will follow this man to the ends of the earth."

So the bargain was struck. The next day the bells rang for the betrothal, and there was a grand feast. Many of the festive dishes were flavored with salt. Everyone ate heartily, especially Marushka.

And all day long Ivan's sailors were busy unloading barrels of salt and heaving onto the deck the barrels of gold and silver and jewels and carrying them down into the hold, where they glimmered in the darkness.

At the last minute, while the tsarevna was embracing her father in farewell, Ivan scooped up a handful of salt and put it in his pocket. Then the sailors hauled up the anchor. The sails rushed up the mast, the flag flew, and away went the ship across the sea, heading for home.

How glad my father will be, thought Ivan, when I bring him gold and silver and precious stones in place of his wooden spoons!

But when they had sailed out of sight of land—not too near, not too far—Ivan saw two sails approaching. He knew them at once. They were the ships of his two brothers, Fyodor and Vasily.

But the ships were sadly changed. Their sails were in shreds. Their hulls were patched and broken. They were wallowing dangerously in the waves.

Ivan called to his brothers to abandon their leaking ships and take refuge in his own. At once they jumped into little boats and rowed across the water to Ivan's ship and scrambled aboard. Their crewmen, too, thin and gaunt from hunger, swam to the ship and clawed their way over the railing.

"Welcome, my brothers," cried Ivan. "But tell me, what has happened to your beautiful ships?"

"There was a storm," growled Fyodor. "It nearly wrecked my ship. It blew me south instead of north. I landed in a hot country where no one wanted my furs. I had to sell them at a loss."

"I, too, was blown off course by the storm," whined Vasily. "My mast was cracked. Before I could make my way to land, my cargo of ice was all melted."

Then Fyodor looked around greedily at the handsome fittings of the little ship. "I see, my foolish brother Ivan, that you, too, have had a turn at trading in our father's goods."

Proudly, Ivan showed them his cargo of gold and silver and jewels. Beaming with joy, he brought forward his betrothed, the tsarevna.

Vasily and Fyodor were envious of his good fortune. They looked at each other and whispered together. Suddenly they seized Ivan and threw him over the side.

Marushka cried out, and she would have jumped after him, but they thrust her into her cabin and locked the door.

Then Fyodor and Vasily argued over Ivan's treasure. At last they agreed that Fyodor should have the gold and silver and Vasily the jewels and the tsar's daughter.

But Marushka would have none of Vasily! "No," she shouted, and then she began to cry for her beloved Ivan.

It was terrible how she cried! Her salt tears ran down her cheeks until the floor of the cabin was awash. They ran out under the door and down the hatches until they filled the hold of the ship. Soon it was sinking lower and lower into the sea.

"Stop crying, Tsarevna," cried Vasily, pounding on her door. "You will sink the ship!"

But she couldn't stop. The ship sank farther and tipped over on its side.

"Throw out your jewels!" cried Fyodor to Vasily.

"Never," shouted Vasily. "Throw out your gold and silver!"

"Throw out the tsarevna!" shrieked Fyodor. "It is her fault the ship is sinking!"

Then Vasily hurled himself at Fyodor, and they fought on the slanting deck. In desperation the sailors picked up the barrels of gold and silver and jewels and threw them overboard. At once the ship righted itself and sailed on.

In the meantime, where was poor Ivan the Fool?

He had not drowned! When his brothers threw him into the sea, he climbed into Fyodor's little boat and tried to reach one of the two ships that had belonged to his brothers. But while he was rowing as hard as he could, there was a terrible creaking and groaning, and both ships disappeared beneath the rolling waves.

Now there was nothing for Ivan to do but row with all his might, hoping to come to some unknown coast. Luckily, he reached an island by evening.

Beaching the little boat, Ivan walked inland. He was very thirsty. In the middle of a forest of lofty trees he found a spring of fresh water. Cupping some in his hands, he drank and drank.

But—poor Ivan. If it wasn't one thing, it was another—the island was the home of a giant! Catching sight of Ivan, the giant reached down, picked him up in his enormous hand, and lifted him up to look at him.

Ivan's head brushed the clouds. Well, he thought dizzily, at least I have found out how high the sky is.

"What a choice morsel," thundered the giant, squeezing Ivan in his hand.

Then Ivan remembered his knife. Whipping it out of his belt, he thrust it into the giant's thumb. But it made only a tiny prick. The giant didn't feel it at all.

"I will swallow you in one gulp," he bellowed, opening his mouth wide.

"Oh, but I will taste better with a little salt," cried Ivan. Quickly he thrust his hand into his pocket, pulled out a handful of salt, and poured it on the place where he had pricked the giant's thumb.

The salt burned. The giant howled with pain. Falling to his knees, he dropped Ivan on the ground. "Help me," he groaned, "and I will do anything you desire."

"No sooner said than done," said Ivan. Dipping water from the spring with his hands, he poured it over the giant's thumb.

At once the pain stopped. The giant stopped howling and glowered at Ivan. "What do you want?" he growled.

"I want you to carry me across the sea," said Ivan.

"Oh, is that all?" Once again the giant picked up Ivan. This time he tucked him in his pocket. Putting one tremendous foot into the sea and then the other, he set off, wading through the water, walking many versts at each step.

"Not this way," cried Ivan. "My home is the other way."

But the giant paid no attention. He walked through the sea all the way around the world, over vast continents and valleys and mountains, carrying Ivan in his pocket, until at last they came to the country Ivan called home.

There the giant set him down.

"Thank you," called Ivan, as the giant plodded back into the water and splashed away across the sea. "Good-bye!"

Well, at least I have discovered that the world is round, not flat, thought Ivan. Eagerly he ran toward his father's house, hoping to find that his wicked brothers had brought Marushka back with them, safe and sound.

And there she was! Looking out the window, she saw him coming. Before he could open the door, Marushka rushed out and threw herself into his arms. She was more beautiful than ever, in a bridal crown and a splendid dress stiff with pearls.

"You have come just in time," cried Marushka. "Today I am to be married to your brother Vasily. Listen, the wedding bells are ringing! Your father would not believe that your brothers threw you overboard and stole your ship. He said his son Ivan was too foolish to win a tsarevna and a cargo of treasure."

Angrily, Ivan strode into the house. There stood his brother Vasily dressed like a bridegroom, and his father and his brother Fyodor in their wedding finery of kaftans with silver buttons.

They were dumbfounded to see Ivan. Had he not drowned at sea after all? "Oh, my poor son," cried his father, embracing him, "why did you stay away so long? Your brothers have been home for many weeks!"

Ivan looked at his brothers, but they were ashamed and would not meet his eyes. "The devil's work is quick," he said, "but God works slowly." Then Ivan took Marushka's hand and turned to his father. "She is my bride, not Vasily's."

"Take her," said Vasily angrily. "What good is a wife who cries from morning till night?"

"Take her," said Ivan's father. "It is terrible how she cries." Then he looked at Ivan's ragged clothes and shook his head. "My foolish son, I see that you, too, have failed. Now there is nothing to show for all my sons' journeys. No gold, no silver, no jewels."

"But, Father, there is something else." Ivan pulled the last of the salt from his pocket and let it trickle through his fingers to the floor. "I know of an island not far away where there is a mountain of salt."

"Salt!" cried the merchant. "Heaven be praised! You have done well, my clever Ivan! From now on we will trade in salt! We will carry salt to the ends of the earth. For salt is more precious than gold. Without salt there is no savor!"

And so Ivan and Marushka were married, and the merchant sent a fleet of ships around the world, carrying the savor of salt to all the lands beyond the sea.

Do you believe my story? Do you believe there really was a ship full of treasure and a tsarevna who nearly sank it with her salt tears and a giant who walked around the earth?

Well, at least I can tell you that the salt tears are true.

The next time you cry, let the tears run down your cheeks and taste them with your tongue. Don't they taste of salt?

The cat has finished the story.
Once again he climbs the tree.
Sitting on a branch,
He switches his tail and sings a song.

Song of Majesty
(Velitchálnaya Pyésnya)

Rimsky-Korsakov

Blue is the o - cean, change-less and bound - less,

vast depths of wa - ter, sun - less and sound - less.

Hail to thee, blue o - cean, _____

change - less and bound - less!